Are You Ready for a

POP QUIZ?

How much do you know about Leonardo DiCaprio? Will you make the grade? Brush up on your Leo trivia and try your hand at these questions:

- Where does Leo like to go when he's on a break from a movie shoot?
- Early in his career, one Hollywood agent suggested Leonardo change his name. What did the agent suggest Leo change his name to?
- In *Titanic,* how does Jack Dawson get his ticket for the ill-fated voyage?

Packed with tons of trivia, a special pull-out poster, and quizzes to test *your* Leonardo knowledge. Find all these answers and more in . . .

Pop Quiz: Leonardo DiCaprio

Look for other celebrity biographies from
Archway Paperbacks

POP QUIZ

LEONARDO DiCAPRIO

NANCY KRULIK

AN ARCHWAY PAPERBACK
Published by POCKET BOOKS
New York   London   Toronto   Sydney   Tokyo   Singapore

AN ARCHWAY PAPERBACK *Original*

An Archway Paperback published by
POCKET BOOKS, a division of Simon & Schuster Inc.
1230 Avenue of the Americas, New York, NY 10020

ISBN: 0-671-02771-9

First Archway Paperback printing November 1998

10 9 8 7 6 5 4 3

AN ARCHWAY PAPERBACK and colophon are
registered trademarks of Simon & Schuster Inc.

Front cover photo and poster photo by Kalpesh Lathigra/FSP/
Liaison International

Printed in the U.S.A.

IL 4+

For Alison Hashmall

CONTENTS

CONTENTS

INTRODUCTION
ARE YOU IN THE KNOW ABOUT DiCAPRIO?

"Everywhere I go, people are staring at me. I don't know if people are staring because they recognize me or because they think I'm a weirdo."

—*Leonardo DiCaprio*

Times sure have changed for Leonardo DiCaprio. A few short months ago he was just one of a huge pack of young Hollywood actors, well-known to a small group of fans, but certainly not a household name. Then, along came a billion-dollar blockbuster called *Titanic*. Suddenly, Leonardo was a major star (if not *the* major star) in Hollywood, and his world turned upside down. TV commentators spent countless hours speculating whether or not he would attend the 1998 Academy Awards show (he did not) and whether or not he would be partying at New York's Chaos club or Moomba restaurant (he often did). Leo couldn't make a move without the cameras following him. He even had to hire bodyguards to accompany him and his friends on their late-night outings.

Despite the considerable disruption to his private life, Leo is extremely thankful to his fans, because he knows that they are the reason he is where he is today. Of his fame, he'll say only that, "It's cool, but we'll see how it goes." But of his fans he says, "They'll never know how grateful I am for their support."

Are you one of the people who can't get enough of Leonardo DiCaprio? Do you collect his pictures and pin them all over your walls? Do you scribble his name on every page of your notebook? Do you rent his movies and have all-night marathon screenings of *This Boy's Life, The Basketball Diaries,* and *Romeo & Juliet*? Were you convinced he was robbed of a Best Actor nomination for *Titanic*? Are you waiting with baited breath for the release of Woody Allen's new movie, *Celebrity,* hoping to catch a glimpse of Leo in a cameo role? Do you keep up-to-date on all things DiCaprio, including his likes and dislikes, and the behind-the-scenes secrets from all of his movies?

If you answered yes to those questions, you qualify as a true DiCaprimaniac—and this book is for you! *Pop Quiz: Leonardo DiCaprio* is filled with questions about the world's hottest heartthrob, Leonardo DiCaprio. Some of the questions are relatively easy—others will take Leo know-how of titanic proportions to answer correctly. (We're not even sure his mother could answer *all* of the questions in this book!) But don't agonize too long over the toughies—you can always check your answers at the end of each section. And don't forget to total your score at the end of the book, just to see how you measure up to other Leo fans.

So what are you waiting for? Turn the page and let the fun begin!

1
LEO'S VITAL STATISTICS

Okay, so you've seen Titanic *twenty times. You've watched every Leo rerun of* Growing Pains. *And as for* The Man in the Iron Mask, *well, you can tell whether Leo's playing Philippe or Louis at a glance. But how much do you know about the* real *Leonardo DiCaprio? Let's get down to the basics and find out.*

1. What is Leo's full real name?

2. What is Leo's nickname?

3. What color are Leo's eyes?

4. How tall is Leo?

5. How much does Leo weigh?

6. True or false: Leo dyes his naturally brown hair blond.

1

7. What is Leo's birthday?

8. What is Leo's birth sign?

9. Where did Leo attend school?

10. What was the name of Leonardo's first date?

11. True or false: Leonardo has two sisters.

12. Where was Leo born?

13. What does Leo consider his worst quality?

14. What is Leo's goal in life?

15. True or false: Leo has quit smoking.

Answers to the Leo's Vital Statistics Quiz

1. Leonardo Wilhelm DiCaprio

2. Noodles

3. Blue-green

4. Six feet tall

5. About 140 pounds

6. False. He's a natural blond.

7. November 11, 1974

8. Scorpio

9. The Center for Enriched Studies and John Marshall High School

10. Cessi

11. False. He is an only child.

12. Hollywood, California

13. He tends to procrastinate.

14. To become a great actor

15. False. (Unfortunately, but he does vow to quit soon.)

2
LEO'S FAMILY TREE

Although Leonardo DiCaprio finally moved out of his mother's house last year, he still visits her pretty often. That's because he misses her. "It's a weird adjustment living alone," he explains, "because you don't realize how much you miss Mumsie until she's not around."

But Leo isn't usually too far from Mom. He often makes the short trip to her house for a home-cooked meal, and takes her with him when he travels to exciting places. She went with him to the New York premiere of *The Man in the Iron Mask*, and stood next to him on the receiving line when Britain's Prince Charles congratulated Leo on his *Titanic* performance.

Leo is also close to his father. Although his parents divorced when he was very young, Leo never felt separated from his dad. The DiCaprios have always shared the responsibilities of raising their son and often took turns taking him to many of his early auditions. Leo's father also always found the time to take his son to comic-book and baseball-card conventions.

"My parents are so a part of my life that they are like my legs or something," Leo has told many reporters.

All of the questions in this quiz are about the people who are closest to Leonardo DiCaprio—his family. How much do you know about the folks who know Leo best?

1. What is Leo's mother's name?

2. In what country was Leo's mother born?

3. What is Leo's father's name?

4. True or false: Leo grew up in Beverly Hills.

5. How old was Leonardo when his parents split up?

6. What did Leo's dad do for a living while Leo was growing up?

7. True or false: When Leo was a baby, his mother modeled for the Sears catalog to make the money she needed to support her young son.

8. What is Leo's stepbrother's name?

9. Leo's stepbrother had a part in a commercial. What product was the commercial for?

10. True or false: Leo never pierced his nose because he was afraid of his father's reaction.

11. True or false: Leo chose his own name when he was eight years old. Before that his name was John DiCaprio.

12. True or false: Leo's parents met in high school.

13. Leonardo's father was once called to the school principal's office because Leo had spent the school day doing an imitation of what mass murderer?

14. Now that Leo is a multimillionaire, who is he building a summerhouse for?

15. True or false: Leo once described his family as "not the hippie family who only eats organic and the children meditate. But we're not apple-pie Republican either."

16. Which two of the following does Leo recall as his favorite childhood memories?

    a) Going on a motorcycle tour with his father
    b) Going to the art museum with his parents

    c) Camping at the Grand Canyon with his mother

    d) Going for pony rides with his mom and dad

17. Leo's first agent was a friend of whom?

18. Why did Leo decide to go into acting?

19. After Leo lost an early acting job, someone told him, "Someday, Leonardo, it will happen for you. Just remember these words." Who was that someone?

20. How old was Leonardo DiCaprio when he finally got his own home?

21. Who, besides his mother, did Leo introduce to Prince Charles?

22. Who helped Leo with his lines while he was on the soap opera *Santa Barbara*?

23. "Hollywood was the place where all this great stuff was going on. Meanwhile, it was a disgusting place to be." According to Leo, which of his parents thought this?

24. True or false: While waiting to hear whether or not he would win the Best Supporting Actor Oscar for his role in *What's Eating Gilbert Grape,* Leo had to deal with helping

his mom get to her seat after a bathroom run.

25. One of Leo's parents declared that Leo was not going to attend the 1998 Academy Awards, saying, "He wasn't nominated. Why should he go?" Which one?

ANSWERS TO THE LEO'S FAMILY TREE QUIZ

1. Irmelin DiCaprio

2. Germany

3. George DiCaprio

4. False. He grew up in Hollywood, California.

5. Less than one year old

6. He created and distributed underground comic books.

7. False. She took on a series of odd jobs.

8. Adam Starr

9. Golden Grahams cereal

10. False. In fact, Leo says, "My dad would welcome it if I got a nose ring."

11. False. Leo was named while his mother was still pregnant with him. She was looking at a painting by artist Leonardo da Vinci when the unborn baby kicked. From that moment on, baby DiCaprio's name was Leonardo.

12. False. They met in college.

13. Charles Manson

14. His mother

15. True

16. b and d

17. His mother

18. To move his mother and himself out of a neighborhood which he describes as "a Hollywood ghetto"

19. His father

20. Twenty-two

21. His grandmother, Helena Indenbirken

22. His parents

23. His mom

24. True. The usher almost refused to allow her back to her seat. But Leo cleared the way for her. Unfortunately, Leo didn't win the award that night.

25. His mom

3
FAVES!

Many fans ask the same question: Now that he's got money, fame, and prestige, is Leonardo truly happy? Well, only Leo can answer that one.

"I'm just starting to scratch the surface of what makes me happy," he says. "It has taken me a while to admit that sometimes acting like a child can be fun."

There are lots of other things that make Leo happy, like roller coasters that go upside down really fast, visiting museums and art galleries, and hanging out on the New York club scene with his friends.

How much do you know about Leo's favorite things (and we're not talking raindrops on roses here)? There's no time like the present to find out.

1. Where does Leo like to go when he's on a break from a movie shoot?

2. What is Leo's favorite color?

3. What is Leo's favorite food?

4. Which of these is *not* one Leo's favorite bands?

   a) The Beatles
   b) Led Zeppelin
   c) Pink Floyd
   d) The Eagles

5. Name Leo's three favorite living actors.

6. Name Leo's favorite basketball team.

7. What is Leo's favorite thing to collect?

8. What is Leo's favorite soft drink?

9. Which does Leo prefer—playing pool or bowling?

10. Name Leonardo's favorite song.

11. Who is Leo's favorite living actress?

12. What is Leonardo's favorite book?

13. True or false: Leonardo's all-time favorite TV show is *The Honeymooners*.

14. True or false: Leo has agreed to star in a bio flick about his favorite 1950s screen idol, James Dean.

15. True or false: Leo loves to go skydiving whenever he can.

16. What is Leo's favorite vacation spot?

17. Leo prefers fictional acting roles to true-life characters.

18. What are Leo's three favorite movies?

19. True or false: Leo says his first kiss was his favorite because it was so romantic.

20. What is Leo's favorite NY clothing store?

21. Which was Leo's favorite birthday?

22. True or false: The thing Leo likes best about himself is his new rose tattoo.

23. Fill in the blank to complete Leo's favorite saying: Pain is temporary. Film is _____.

24. True or false: Leo likes when his friends call him Leonard.

25. What are Leo's two favorite U.S. cities?

ANSWERS TO THE FAVES QUIZ

1. To the beach. He likes to watch the waves roll in.

2. Green. "It's the color of nature, the color of money, and the color of moss," he explains.

3. Pasta

4. d

5. Robert De Niro, Jack Nicholson, and Al Pacino

6. The Los Angeles Lakers

7. Five-dollar sunglasses

8. Lemonade

9. Playing pool. And he's very good. Some of his friends say he can be a real pool shark when he wants to.

10. Otis Redding's "Sittin' on the Dock of the Bay"

11. Meg Ryan

12. *The Old Man and the Sea* by Ernest Hemingway

13. False. It's *The Twilight Zone.*

14. False

15. It's true. Leo loves the excitement of the sport. In fact, the first time he went skydiving his chute didn't open correctly. His instructor had to pull the emergency cord to keep Leo from plummeting to his death. But that experience didn't keep Leo from jumping again.

16. Germany

17. False. He often prefers nonfiction characters because "a lot of the time, real-life people can be a hundred times more interesting than any stories writers can create in their heads."

18. *The Godfather, The Godfather: Part II,* and *The Godfather: Part III*

19. False. In fact he says it was disgusting. (Luckily, over the years, his love life has gotten better.)

20. Barney's

21. His sixteenth birthday, because he got his driver's license.

22. False. It's his sense of humor. Leo says he probably will never get a tattoo. Not because

he's vain, but because he doesn't feel he'd like
to do something permanent to his body.

23. Forever

24. False. He hates it when people call him that!

25. New York and San Francisco

4
MEET THE CO-STARS

One thing is for sure—Leo is loved by his fellow performers. He's fun to be around on the set, whether he's copying Michael Jackson's moon-walk dance moves, or imitating the idiosyncrasies of his fellow cast mates. Leonardo is also a notoriously generous actor, who is more worried about the scene as a whole than about how he looks in the shot.

Leo's worked with some of the best actors in the world, including Academy Award winners Robert De Niro, Meryl Streep, and Diane Keaton, as well as with up-and-coming superstars like Claire Danes, Mark Wahlberg, and Kate Winslet.

How much do you know about Leo's co-stars? There's only one way to find out—answer these trivia questions!

1. Which of Leo's co-stars once said of him, "I spent four months on the set with [Leo] and

couldn't figure out whether he's transparent or incredibly complex"?

2. According to Leo, which of his female co-stars kissed him like he was a kid?

3. Kate Winslet sent something to *Titanic* director James Cameron along with a note that read, "You don't understand. I am Rose. I don't know why you're even seeing anyone else." What did she send him?

4. Which of Leo's co-stars used her own money to pay his salary for a film she produced?

5. What two films did Juliette Lewis appear in with Leo?

6. What two movies featured both Leonardo DiCaprio and Robert De Niro?

7. Which of Leo's co-stars once said of him, "He didn't listen to me at all—and I'm his mother"?

8. Which of Leo's leading ladies once had the nickname Blubber?

9. Which of Leo's co-stars accepted the Nickelodeon Kids' Choice award on behalf of the cast and crew of *Titanic*?

10. *Vanity Fair* chose two of Leo's leading ladies to be photographed with a group of young actresses who the staff of the magazine believed had huge careers in front of them. Name these two stars.

11. Which co-star does Leo credit with teaching him how to deal with fame?

12. Which of Leo's TV co-stars once said of him, "He's a great actor who will do great movies"?

13. Leo once described working with one of his co-stars as "going to acting school every day." Name the actor.

14. One of Leo's directors once told him point-blank, "Look, I'm not going to make this guy brooding and neurotic. I'm not going to give [the character] a tic and a limp and all those things you want!" Name this straightforward director.

15. Which of Leo's leading ladies once described him as "one of the most loyal people I know"?

16. Which of Leo's co-stars began his career as a rap singer?

17. Leo had a tiny role in an early 1980s movie. It starred *Roseanne*'s Sarah Gilbert and the star of *E.T.* Name the movie and the former child star.

18. Who played Leo's sick aunt in *Marvin's Room*?

19. Which of Leo's leading ladies said of him, "When he's acting you can't watch anything else"?

20. Which of Leo's leading ladies called him, "Probably the most beautiful looking man—and yet he doesn't know he's gorgeous"?

Answers to the Meet the Co-stars Quiz

1. Claire Danes

2. Sharon Stone

3. A single red rose

4. Sharon Stone, who both starred in and produced *The Quick and the Dead*

5. *What's Eating Gilbert Grape* and *The Basketball Diaries*

6. *This Boy's Life* and *Marvin's Room*

7. Meryl Streep, who played Leo's mother in *Marvin's Room*

8. Kate Winslet

9. Billy Zane

10. Claire Danes and Kate Winslet

11. Kirk Cameron from the TV show *Growing Pains*

12. Tracey Gold

13. Robert De Niro

14. James Cameron. (He was talking about the role of Jack Dawson.)

15. Claire Danes

16. Mark (Marky Mark) Wahlberg

17. *Poison Ivy*, starring Drew Barrymore. Leo's role was so small it didn't have name. He was just Guy #1.

18. Diane Keaton

19. Meryl Streep

20. Kate Winslet

5
LEO GEO(GRAPHY)

Some people like working in an office. They enjoy the security of knowing that they will be going to the same place day after day, and being around people they know well.

Leo, however, is not one of those people. He enjoys the ever-changing atmosphere of an actor's life. One month he can be in Mexico finishing up a film, and the very next month he may find himself in Paris, starting a new one.

All that traveling is just fine with Leo. In fact, he wishes he could do more traveling. His hope is to someday take a year off and travel around the world. "I want to experience everything that's going on in the United States and overseas," he told one reporter.

Here's your chance to see how much you know about the stamps on Leo's passport. Can you figure out where in the world is Leonardo DiCaprio?

1. While shooting *The Basketball Diaries,* Leo and his co-star, Mark Wahlberg, were seen haunting the club scene in which U.S. city?

2. While on location with *Romeo & Juliet,* one of Leo's friends wound up getting in a fight and having a rib broken. Another of his pals was kidnapped by a taxi driver in the same city. In what metropolis did all of this mayhem occur?

3. In what city did *Titanic* make its world premiere?

4. Which of these New York clubs is Leo often spotted in?

    a) Chaos
    b) The Limelight
    c) The China Club

5. In which country did James Cameron construct the giant water tank used for the filming of *Titanic?*

6. In which romantic city was *The Man in the Iron Mask* filmed?

7. True or false: *Growing Pains* was filmed on Long Island, New York.

8. True or false: *Romeo & Juliet* was originally scheduled to be shot in South Beach, Miami, Florida.

9. Recently Leo joined an unofficial artistic entourage (which also included singer Alanis Morissette) on a visit to what country?

10. Where was Leo reportedly holed up on the night of the 1998 Academy Awards show?

11. Where does Leo work out when he's in Los Angeles?

12. Leo met Britain's Prince Charles at the UK premiere of which film?

13. True or false: As is the custom, Prince Charles shook hands with Leo and moved on, without ever saying a word.

14. True or false: Leonardo was mugged while promoting *The Man in the Iron Mask* at the Cannes Film Festival in 1998.

15. In what famous theater did *The Man in the Iron Mask* premiere?

16. When Leo was cast as Tobias Wolff in *This Boy's Life*, he made a visit to the town where the real

Tobias attended high school. Where did Tobias Wolff go to high school?

17. What state was Leo in when he had his now-famous skydiving incident in which his chute didn't open, and he almost didn't make it?

18. Leonardo donated five thousand dollars in order to have dinner with President Bill Clinton at a fund-raiser in which city?

19. In which trendy California store can Leo often be found buying clothes?

20. Principal photography for *This Boy's Life* took place in which Canadian city?

21. In which Arizona city was *The Quick and the Dead* filmed?

22. Leo has become quite an art collector. In what area of New York City can he often be found haunting the galleries in search of paintings?

23. *Total Eclipse* was filmed in what country?

24. What language (besides English) does Leo speak fluently?

25. True or false: Leonardo traveled to Colorado to film *The Outsiders* movie.

ANSWERS TO THE LEO GEO(GRAPHY) QUIZ

1. New York City

2. Mexico City

3. Tokyo, Japan

4. a

5. Mexico

6. Paris

7. False. Although the series took place in a New York City suburb, it was filmed in California.

8. True. But high production costs forced the shoot out of the country.

9. Cuba

10. In a hotel room in New York City

11. Gold's Gym

12. *Titanic*

13. False. In fact, he actually engaged Leo in a lengthy conversation.

14. False. He wasn't even there.

15. New York's Ziegfeld Theater

16. Concrete, Washington

17. California

18. New York

19. Fred Segal

20. Vancouver

21. Mescal

22. Soho

23. France

24. German

25. False. Leo wasn't in that movie. He appeared in the short lived TV series that was based on the movie. The series was taped in California

6
TUBE TIME!

Leonardo has become such a huge movie star that it is easy to forget that he started his career on the small screen, not the big one. Leo's first acting job came when he was just five years old. He was hired to play a child on a kiddie show called *Romper Room*. Leo's job was to be a normal kid spending a day in a TV classroom. But Leo never made it on camera. He was fired his very first day for disruptive behavior. It would be nine years before he tried acting again.

Okay, now sit back, pick up your remote and press on. It's time for some Leo TV!

1. Early in Leo's career, one Hollywood agent suggested Leo change his name. What did the agent suggest Leo change his name to?

2. Leo's first commercial was for what toy company?

3. What soap opera did Leo appear on?

4. His character on the soap opera in question 3 had a very serious problem. What was it?

5. What did Leo say was the most difficult part of being on a soap opera?

6. True or false: Child actors are limited in the number of hours they can work per day.

7. Leo appeared on two TV series that were based on movies. Name both series.

8. What was the name of Leo's character on *Parenthood*?

9. On which night of the week and at what time was *Parenthood* originally broadcast?

10. How many regular cast members were there on *Parenthood*?

    a) 21 b) 3 c) 15

11. What did Leo have in common with his character on *Parenthood*?

12. When *Parenthood* made Leo a teen idol, who jumped in to handle his publicity?

13. What other movie actor played Leo's brother-in-law on *Parenthood*?

14. Name Leonardo's character on *Growing Pains*.

15. Leo's *Growing Pains* character had a very serious problem. What was it?

16. Before Leo joined the *Growing Pains* cast, who was considered the heartthrob of the show?

17. True or false: Leo did not join the cast of *Growing Pains* until the show's last season.

18. Match the *Growing Pains* cast members to their characters:

    a. Alan Thicke   1. Mike
    b. Joanna Kerns   2. Ben
    c. Kirk Cameron   3. Carol
    d. Tracey Gold   4. Maggie
    e. Jeremy Miller   5. Jason
    f. Ashley Johnson   6. Chrissy

19. When Leo got the call that he had landed his role on *Growing Pains*, what did he do to celebrate?

20. *Growing Pains* originally aired on what network?

21. What cable network recently aired all of the *Growing Pains* episodes that featured Leonardo?

22. Which two members of the *Growing Pains* cast eventually married each other?

23. What TV series was a spin-off from *Growing Pains*?

24. Which *Growing Pains* actor does Leo credit with teaching him how to "pick up women"?

25. Which two *Growing Pains* cast members were infamous for their practical jokes?

26. Why did Leo leave *Growing Pains*?

27. How many *Growing Pains* episodes were filmed after Leo left the show?

28. In what year was *Growing Pains* canceled?

29. Who did Leo call "a nice charming guy who knows how to weasel his way out of things"?

30. Since *Growing Pains*, Leo has done more TV work, but not in the U.S. Where can you catch Leo on the tube today?

ANSWERS TO THE TUBE TIME QUIZ

1. Lenny Williams

2. Matchbox Toys

3. *Santa Barbara*

4. He was an alcoholic.

5. Learning all the lines

6. True

7. *The Outsiders* and *Parenthood*

8. Garry Buckman

9. Saturdays at 8:00

10. c

11. They both had divorced parents.

12. Leo's mom

13. David Arquette

14. Luke Brower

15. He was homeless.

16. Kirk Cameron

17. True

18. a-5, b-4, c-1, d-3, e-2, f-6

19. He went out and bought an eighty-dollar pair of shoes.

20. ABC

21. The Disney Channel

22. Kirk Cameron and Chelsea Noble (who played Mike's girlfriend on the show)

23. *Just the Ten of Us*

24. Alan Thicke

25. Kirk Cameron and Jeremy Miller

26. To film *This Boy's Life*

27. Four

28. 1992

29. Luke Brower, his character on *Growing Pains*

30. In Japan. He made a rumored $4 million to do two Suzuki car commercials.

7
Critters 3

When Leo got word that his TV series *Parenthood* was being canceled, he went on the lookout for more work. This time he wanted to do something really different. So, when the offer came to play the lead in a horror flick called *Critters 3*, he jumped at the chance.

Leo probably jumped too soon. *Critters 3* was different from *Parenthood*, that's for sure. The TV series got good critical reviews. *Critters 3*, on the other hand, was an all-out bomb!

Not many people saw Critters 3 *when it was originally in theaters. But since Leo's titanic success, the film has had a resurgence on tape. Are you one of those diehard fans who has actually sat through all of* Critters 3? *Then you won't have any trouble answering these trivia questions. The rest of you may learn a thing or two.*

1. The first movie in the *Critters* series was just called *Critters*. What was the second *Critters* movie called?

2. In *Critters 3*, what causes one of the critters to bubble when it is hacked in the back with a meat cleaver?

3. Who played Leo's dad in *Critters 3*?

4. In what year did Leo make *Critters 3*?

5. Who played the young girl who enlists Leonardo's aid to kill off the critters?

6. Name the director of *Critters 3*.

7. Who called *Critters 3* "possibly one of the worst films of all time"?

8. How many *Critters* films came out after *Critters 3*?

9. What is the name of Leo's character in *Critters 3*?

10. True or false: *Critters 3* takes place in a campground.

ANSWERS TO THE *CRITTERS 3* Quiz

1. *Critters 2: The Main Course*

2. The dish washing detergent it has eaten

3. William Dennis Hunt

4. 1991

5. Aimee Brooks

6. Kristine Peterson

7. Leonardo DiCaprio

8. One, *Critters 4*

9. Josh

10. False. It takes place in a rundown apartment building.

8
THIS BOY'S LIFE

Back in 1992, every young actor in Hollywood wanted to be in *This Boy's Life* because it meant the chance to work with Robert De Niro. Every young actor except Leonardo, that is. Sure he wanted to be in *This Boy's Life* because he felt the character of Toby was wonderfully written. But Leo wasn't really familiar with De Niro's films or the powerful presence he had in Hollywood.

"My ignorance was sort of an advantage," Leo explained to a *Vanity Fair* reporter. "[At the audition] I stood up in front of De Niro really forcefully and I pointed at his face and screamed one of the lines. The cool thing is, I really showed him something."

Leo got the part, and he was soon in awe of De Niro's talents. By the time the film was over, the rest of the world was in awe of Leo's talents. Some people felt Leo actually stole the film from Robert De Niro. (Not bad praise for the new kid on the block!) One thing was certain, however— the minute the movie was released, this boy's life was never going to be the same.

1. Where was Leonardo when he heard he had gotten the role in *This Boy's Life*?

2. Leo was so happy to hear he had gotten the part in *This Boy's Life* that he did something very odd (and a little violent). What did he do?

3. How many actors did Leonardo beat out to get his role in *This Boy's Life*?

   a) more than 20
   b) more than 150
   c) more than 400

4. *This Boy's Life* is the true story of what author?

5. Who played Leo's mom in *This Boy's Life*?

6. Name the director of *This Boy's Life*.

7. True or false: Leo had a supporting role in *This Boy's Life*.

8. In what state does *This Boy's Life* take place?

9. Which of the three leading actors in *This Boy's Life* did the director consider "the rock that this movie is built on"?

10. *This Boy's Life* takes place in what decade?

ANSWERS TO THE *THIS BOY'S LIFE* Quiz

1. On vacation in Germany with his mother

2. He punched a hole in the ceiling.

3. c

4. Tobias Wolff

5. Ellen Barkin

6. Michael Caton-Jones

7. False. He was a full-fledged star. In fact, he was in almost every scene of the movie.

8. Washington

9. Leonardo DiCaprio

10. The 1950s

9
WHAT'S EATING GILBERT GRAPE

How do you follow up rave reviews in a Robert De Niro movie? Get yourself an Oscar-worthy supporting role in a film which stars one of Hollywood's red-hot actors, that's how! That's just what Leo did when he took on the role of Arnie Grape in *What's Eating Gilbert Grape*. Arnie Grape was completely different than Tobias Wolff. For starters, Arnie was mentally disabled. That proved to be a real challenge to Leo because he was determined not to turn Arnie into a caricature.

Leo spent a lot of time with mentally challenged young people in order to study their mannerisms and to try and get some insight into their feelings. All that research really paid off: Leo received an Academy Award nomination for his portrayal of Arnie Grape.

Is your knowledge of What's Eating Gilbert Grape *trivia worthy of an award? To find out, answer the questions below.*

1. What was the name of Arnie Grape's older brother?

2. Who played Arnie Grape's older brother?

3. Why did Lasse Hallström (the movie's director) say that he chose Leonardo for the role of Arnie Grape?

4. In the movie, what finally forced Arnie's mom to leave the house?

5. What kind of special prosthesis did Leonardo wear to give Arnie a slightly deformed look?

6. Why was Arnie's big brother ashamed of his mom?

7. What birthday is coming up for Arnie in *What's Eating Gilbert Grape*?

8. What happens to the Grape family's house at the end of the movie?

9. Where does Arnie Grape like to climb to?

10. Where does Arnie Grape's older brother work?

11. What restaurant opens up in town during the movie?

12. What movie did Leonardo turn down to do *What's Eating Gilbert Grape?*

13. What famous agency did Leonardo sign with after acting in *What's Eating Gilbert Grape?*

14. True or false: Leo has called portraying Arnie Grape "some of the most fun I've ever had."

15. Who won the Best Supporting Actor award the year Leo was nominated?

ANSWERS TO THE
WHAT'S EATING GILBERT GRAPE Quiz

1. Gilbert

2. Johnny Depp

3. He liked the distance in his eyes.

4. Arnie was arrested.

5. A special mouthpiece

6. She was obese.

7. His eighteenth

8. It burns down.

9. To the top of the town water tower

10. Lamson's Grocery Store

11. Burger Barn

12. *Hocus Pocus*

13. CAA (Creative Artists Agency)

14. True

15. Tommy Lee Jones for *The Fugitive*

10
THE BASKETBALL DIARIES

One thing is for sure, as an actor, Leonardo DiCaprio does not ever take the easy way out. While he could have constantly chosen roles that would keep him on the romantic-lead A-list, he has opted for playing human beings with great faults—people who have to reach rock bottom before clawing their way back up to the top.

New York poet Jim Carroll is one such man. Jim was a heroin abuser who later kicked the habit and became an award-winning writer. *The Basketball Diaries* is Jim's story.

Playing a living person is hard enough, but playing a living person with an addiction is even harder. So, in order to make the character of Jim believable, Leo worked closely with a drug counselor to discuss the effects of certain drugs on the body.

"I knew the basics [of what drug use does to your mind and body], but I relied on a drug counselor to learn about specific behavioral nuances," he explains.

And learn them he did. In fact, Leo was so convincing on screen as a heroin abuser, that the press began to speculate as to whether or not Leonardo himself was actually on drugs. Of course, Leonardo assured his fans that those rumors were totally untrue!

It's time for you to take to the court and try your hand at these Basketball Diaries *questions. Ready? Play ball!*

1. What powdered drink (which looked remarkably like heroin on-camera) did the cast of *The Basketball Diaries* sniff during their drug-taking scenes?

2. What is the name of Mark Wahlberg's *Basketball Diaries* character?

3. What disease does Jim's friend Bobby die from in the movie?

4. How old is Bobby when he dies?

5. Into what river do Jim and his friends go diving?

6. Which of his parents does Jim live with?

7. What *When Harry Met Sally* actor plays Jim's basketball coach in *The Basketball Diaries*?

8. What underwear company did Mark Wahlberg model for before joining the cast of *The Basketball Diaries*?

9. Mark Wahlberg's brother Donny was part of what famous singing group?

10. What music-video director directed *The Basketball Diaries*?

11. *The Basketball Diaries* takes place at the beginning of which decade?

12. While he's in the hospital, Bobby asks to read something Jim has in his pocket. What is it?

13. What does Jim give Bobby as a gift from the team?

14. How much jail time did Jim get sentenced to for possession of narcotics, assault, robbery, and resisting arrest?

15. How many versions of *The Basketball Diaries* script were written before the film finally went into production?

ANSWERS TO *THE BASKETBALL DIARIES* Quiz

1. Ovaltine

2. Mickey

3. Leukemia

4. Sixteen

5. The Harlem River

6. His mother

7. Bruno Kirby

8. Calvin Klein

9. New Kids on the Block

10. Scott Kalvert. Scott had previously directed some of Mark Wahlberg's music videos.

11. The 1960s

12. Poetry

13. A signed basketball from a game their team won

14. Six months

15. Ten scripts over a period of fifteen years

11
TOTAL ECLIPSE

In France, poet Arthur Rimbaud is known as a true rebel—a regular James Dean. And since James Dean is Leo's all-time idol, it came as no surprise to his family that Leo agreed to play Rimbaud in *Total Eclipse*—even though the film included some nudity and a scene in which Leo had to kiss another man.

Total Eclipse was not a huge hit for Leo, but the role of Rimbaud did strike a chord with the young actor. As Leo explains, "[Rimbaud] was one of the first rebels. He revolutionized poetry at the age of sixteen!" At the time he was making *Total Eclipse,* young Leo was already revolutionizing the cinema.

Playing Rimbaud was difficult for Leo, because the rebellious poet had little or no consideration for anyone else. That's very unlike the kind and caring Leonardo. But Leo pulled off the part quite convincingly, and he feels it marked a turning point in his career.

"The role of Rimbaud is one of the most important of my career," he declares, "and one of the best roles to play for a young actor."

Are you ready to leave your mark like Rimbaud did? Then try your hand at these tough Total Eclipse *questions.*

1. Who is Paul Verlaine?

2. Is Rimbaud older or younger than the poet he is in love with?

3. At the beginning of *Total Eclipse,* what does Rimbaud send to Verlaine, which inspires Verlaine to invite Rimbaud to his home?

4. What is the name of Verlaine's pregnant wife?

5. What does Verlaine do to his wife's hair?

6. Name the actor who played Verlaine.

7. How old is Rimbaud at the beginning of *Total Eclipse?*

8. Where did Rimbaud go after leaving France while Verlaine was in jail?

9. While *Total Eclipse* writer Christopher Hampton was a student at Oxford University, what did he study?

10. True or false: The film *Total Eclipse* is based on a play.

11. When *Total Eclipse* was first released it was compared to what other film about an eccentric but brilliant artist?

12. Who helped convince Leo to take the role of Rimbaud?

13. *Total Eclipse* takes place in which decade?

    a) 1730s b) 1870s c) 1920s

14. At the same time Leo was deciding to take the Rimbaud role in *Total Eclipse,* he was thinking of playing another rebellious artist in a biographical movie. Who was that other artist?

15. How old was Arthur Rimbaud when he died?

ANSWERS TO THE *TOTAL ECLIPSE* Quiz

1. A poet and Rimbaud's lover in *Total Eclipse*

2. Younger

3. Some of his poems

4. Mathilde

5. He sets it on fire.

6. David Thewlis

7. Nineteen

8. Africa

9. The poetry and life of Arthur Rimbaud

10. True. Christopher Hampton wrote the play when he was 18. The play and screenplay were based on the letters and poems of Paul Verlaine and Arthur Rimbaud.

11. *Amadeus,* which is about composer Wolfgang Amadeus Mozart

12. Author Jim Carroll, whom Leo portrayed in *The Basketball Diaries*

13. b

14. James Dean. Leo now says he probably won't ever play James Dean in the movies.

15. Thirty-seven

12
THE QUICK AND THE DEAD

Most little boys play cowboy at one time or another—using their fingers as toy guns to shoot each other at a showdown on a make-believe main street. But very few little boys get the opportunity to play the game again once they are all grown up. That's one of the benefits of being an actor—you get to play make-believe all the time.

Taking a role in *The Quick and the Dead* was not a decision that came easily to Leonardo. He wasn't sure that a western was the best move for his career. "I had this thing about not doing big commercial movies," he explains. But when he discovered that Sharon Stone and Gene Hackman had signed on, Leo figured the film couldn't miss.

Leo was wrong. Sharon Stone's core audience just didn't believe her as a gun-toting member of the Wild West, and they stayed away from the theaters in droves. Still, Leo put on a strong performance. Once again, he had proven he could hold his own with the big guys.

Can you hold your own with the top Leo fans by answering these questions?

1. What is the name of Sharon Stone's character in *The Quick and the Dead*?

2. Who plays Herod in *The Quick and the Dead*?

3. What is Herod's job?

4. Who played the Kid in the movie?

5. The Kid believes that Herod is related to him. What does he believe the relationship to be?

6. How may cents out of every dollar does Herod demand of the citizens of Redemption?

7. True or False: Simon Moore, who wrote the screenplay for *The Quick and the Dead*, was born in Montana.

8. Why does Sharon Stone's character come to Redemption?

9. Who does the Kid fall in love with?

10. What kind of tournament does Herod run in Redemption every year?

11. Who kisses the Kid?

12. Who kills the Kid?

13. What legendary Wild West personality did Leo compare his *The Quick and the Dead* character to?

14. In *The Quick and the Dead,* what was Cort studying to be before Herod calls him back to town?

15. What two skills did Leo study so that he could accurately portray a Wild West gunslinger?

ANSWERS TO *THE QUICK AND THE DEAD* Quiz

1. Ellen

2. Gene Hackman

3. He's the mayor of the town of Redemption.

4. Leonardo DiCaprio

5. He believes Herod is his father.

6. Fifty

7. False. He's British, and he wrote the screen-play without ever stepping foot in the American west.

8. To kill Herod, the man who murdered her father

9. Ellen

10. A quick-draw tournament, where the last man left alive wins the prize

11. Ellen

12. Herod

13. Billy the Kid

14. A priest

15. Martial arts and gun handling

13
WILLIAM SHAKESPEARE'S
ROMEO & JULIET

When director Baz Luhrmann first approached Leonardo about playing Romeo in a new movie version of Shakespeare's romantic play, Leo did not hesitate to give him an answer—no way! Leo didn't feel that Romeo was his kind of role. In his mind, Romeo was the stereotypical soft teen lover, something Leo just couldn't get into. "I was afraid I would look like a fuffy," Leo explains.

It wasn't until Baz convinced Leo that this *Romeo & Juliet* was out to break the stereotypes did Leo agree to take on the role.

"Our version seemed to me more violent and far less romantic," Leo says, explaining how the movie differs from previous versions of *Romeo & Juliet*.

Wherefore art thou Romeo & Juliet *fans? You're needed to answer a few questions.*

1. What did Leo refuse to wear in the movie?

2. *Romeo & Juliet* director Baz Luhrmann was quoted as saying that Leo symbolized what?

3. According to Leo, filming *Romeo & Juliet* was like going to what?

4. In a 1996 *Premiere* magazine interview, Leo's Juliet, Claire Danes, handed him a gift. What was it?

5. At a screening of *Romeo & Juliet*, the fans screamed so loudly whenever Leo was on the screen that his co-star, John Leguizamo, compared Leo to what 1960s rock band?

6. What two awards did Leonardo win for his portrayal of Romeo?

7. Which film version of *Romeo & Juliet* had Leo seen prior to being cast as Romeo?

8. After long days of filming, what game did the cast of *Romeo & Juliet* often gather in Leonardo's room to play?

9. On what cable network can you now catch reruns of Claire Danes's TV show, *My So-Called Life?*

10. Which cast member described *Romeo & Juliet* by saying, "The feelings are so extreme: falling in love for the first time, being trapped by your parents and by the rest of society"?

11. Had Leonardo ever read *Romeo & Juliet* before making the movie?

12. The play *Romeo & Juliet* takes place in Verona. Where does the 1996 film version take place?

13. What do the Montagues and Capulets use instead of swords in *William Shakespeare's Romeo & Juliet*?

14. What song by the Artist Formerly Known as Prince is sung by a church choir in the movie?

15. Would Leo ever take his life for the woman he loved like Romeo did?

ANSWERS TO THE *WILLIAM SHAKESPEARE'S ROMEO & JULIET* Quiz

1. Tights

2. His generation

3. Shakespeare camp

4. Two chocolate eggs in a white paper bag. She'd scribbled the words "Don't ever say I didn't give you anything" on the bag.

5. The Beatles

6. The Blockbuster Award for Favorite Romance Actor and the Silver Berlin Bear Award for Best Actor from the 47th Berlin International Film Festival

7. The Zeffirelli version

8. Taboo

9. MTV

10. Claire Danes

11. Yes, in Junior High

12. Verona Beach

13. Guns

14. "When Doves Cry"

15. He says no. "I wouldn't go as far as he did," he claims. "I simply don't have the guts."

14
MARVIN'S ROOM

Back when Leonardo DiCaprio was just starting out, he made a lot of guest appearances on TV shows like *Lassie, The Outsiders,* and *Roseanne.* His characters were all troubled teens.

The movie *Marvin's Room* threw Leo back into that type of character once again. This time he played Hank, a troubled young man whom his mother has had put away in a mental institution.

Marvin's Room brought Leo back together with his old mentor, Robert De Niro, and placed him in the company of two other Hollywood legends— Diane Keaton and Meryl Streep. As expected, Leo held his own and received good reviews.

Now it's time for you to visit with Aunt Bessie, Grandfather Marvin, Lee, Hank, and Charlie. Pull up a chair and take this Marvin's Room *quiz.*

1. How many scenes do Leo and Robert De Niro share in *Marvin's Room*?

2. What disease does Hank's Aunt Bessie have?

3. Discussing one of his *Marvin's Room* co-stars, Leo said, "I've never seen anyone act the way she does. She's completely spontaneous. She has such a way-out-there way of doing lines, but it works . . . She's a master." Who was he talking about?

4. Who plays Hank's Aunt Bessie in *Marvin's Room*?

5. How does Hank's mother support her two boys, Hank and Charlie?

6. Why do Hank, his brother, and his mother go to see Bessie?

7. What relation is Lee to Hank?

8. True or false: *Marvin's Room* was based on the play of the same name.

9. In what state does Bessie live?

10. Where does Hank's mother promise to take her boys on vacation?

11. Who plays Dr. Wally in *Marvin's Room*?

12. What gift does Bessie give Hank?

13. What has Bessie been doing since her sister left town?

14. In what state do Hank and his family live?

15. Who plays Hank's younger brother Charlie in *Marvin's Room*?

ANSWERS TO THE *MARVIN'S ROOM* Quiz

1. One

2. Leukemia

3. Meryl Streep

4. Diane Keaton

5. She's a hairdresser.

6. To be tested as possible bone marrow donors to help cure her disease

7. She is Hank's mother.

8. True

9. Florida

10. To Walt Disney World

11. Robert De Niro

12. Some tools

13. Taking care of her father

14. Ohio

15. Hal Scardino

15
TITANIC

We could dive into the history of Titanic *(how it cost more to make than any movie ever made, how tough director James Cameron can be to work with, how long the shoot in Mexico was . . .), but by now you know all that. So let's just cut to the chase and give you the chance to show off your stuff by answering these* Titanic *questions.*

1. How does Jack Dawson get his ticket for the *Titanic* voyage?

2. What kind of car do Rose and Jack eventually find themselves in?

3. What is Jack Dawson's profession?

4. How do Jack and Rose meet?

5. Why is Rose going to America?

6. What did Kate Winslet give Leo after the long, cold, wet *Titanic* shoot?

7. James Cameron had a giant tank built for the shooting of *Titanic*. How many gallons of water did the tank hold?

8. Everyone knows Leo was not nominated for an Academy Award for his role as Jack Dawson. But what Best Male Performance award *did* he win for the film?

9. True or false: Leo and Kate Winslet wear the same size shoes.

10. How many Oscars did *Titanic* win?

11. True or false: Leo was James Cameron's first choice for the role of Jack.

12. Who played "the Unsinkable" Molly Brown in *Titanic*?

13. How does Rose get the attention of the rescue boat?

14. True or false: *Titanic* cost more than $300 million to make.

15. Name the two actresses that played Rose.

16. Who has Jack arrested in *Titanic*?

17. In the movie's opening scenes, what do divers discover locked in a safe, decades after the *Titanic* went down?

18. How long does *Titanic* run?

19. Name the four Golden Globe awards won by *Titanic*.

20. At what famous theater did *Titanic* have its Hollywood premiere?

ANSWERS TO THE *TITANIC* QUIZ

1. He wins it in a card game.

2. A Rolls-Royce

3. He's an artist.

4. He rescues her from jumping off the ship.

5. To get married

6. A thermal blanket

7. 17 million

8. The 1998 MTV Movie Award

9. True

10. Eleven

11. False. "He didn't strike me as necessarily having the qualities I wanted for my Jack," Cameron says, adding, "but I met him and basically just loved him. The second I met him I was convinced."

12. Kathy Bates

13. She blows a whistle.

14. False. But it did cost more than $200 million.

15. Kate Winslet and Gloria Stuart

16. Rose's fiancé

17. A drawing of Rose done by Jack Dawson

18. Three hours, fourteen minutes

19. Best Motion Picture, Drama; Best Director (Motion Picture), James Cameron; Best Original Score (Motion Picture), James Horner; Best Original Song (Motion Picture), "My Heart Will Go On" by James Horner and Will Jennings

20. Mann's Chinese Theater

16
THE MAN IN THE IRON MASK

You remember the Three Musketeers don't you? They're the ones who vowed "All for one and one for all!" Well, in *The Man in the Iron Mask*, the threesome is back—they're just a little older.

The Man in the Iron Mask was Leo's follow-up to *Titanic*. And what a great follow-up it was. When Leo woke up on the morning of March 16, he learned that he had broken a cinema record. He was the first leading actor in history to have two number-one movies at the same time (*The Man in the Iron Mask* and *Titanic* had tied for box-office honors over the weekend)!

Although *The Man in the Iron Mask* didn't make the kind of mega money *Titanic* did (what movie could?!), the film's success cemented Leo's place as a major Hollywood player. His asking price for a movie is now rumored to have risen to $20 million dollars.

Now, put down your swords and grab a pencil. This swashbuckling quiz is a battle of the wits.

1. Which King Louis did Leo portray in *The Man in the Iron Mask?*

2. What other character did Leo play in the film?

3. Name the only Musketeer who remains in the service of the king when *The Man in the Iron Mask* opens.

4. Randall Wallace directed and wrote the script for *The Man in the Iron Mask.* He also earned Oscar and Golden Globe nominations for the stirring screenplay he wrote for a Mel Gibson film that Leo greatly admires. Name the film.

5. What is the number of the prisoner who wears the iron mask?

6. What is the name of Athos's son?

7. Which Musketeer has become a priest at the beginning of *The Man in the Iron Mask?*

8. Name the *Green Card* star who plays wild man Porthos.

9. Which brother tells Christine, "I did not mean to hurt you; I will undo any wrong I have done to you"?

10. Finish the quote from the movie: "You will hunt down Porthos, Athos, and Aramis, and bring me their heads . . . or _____."

11. Where did Randall Wallace drive to in order to discuss *The Man in the Iron Mask* with Leo?

12. Who wrote the original novel *The Man in the Iron Mask*?

13. What lucky lady starred opposite Leo as the king's love interest in *The Man in the Iron Mask*?

14. What star of *La Femme Nikita* played Leo's mother in the film?

15. Who was the king's real father?

Answers to *The Man in the Iron Mask* Quiz

1. Louis XIV

2. Philippe (the man in the iron mask)

3. D'Artagnan

4. *Braveheart*

5. 64389000

6. Raoul

7. Aramis

8. Gérard Depardieu

9. Philippe (disguised as his brother the king)

10. I will have yours

11. To Mexico, where Leo was shooting *Titanic*

12. Alexandre Dumas

13. Judith Godrèche

14. Anne Parillaud

15. D'Artagnan

17
SOUND BITES

If you think about the movies Leo has been in, it's hard to find a common thread. His career spans every genre: from a horror movie like *Critters 3*, to a black comedy like *What's Eating Gilbert Grape*, to an epic love story like *Titanic*.

But believe it or not, all of Leo's movies do have something in common. Each one is an exceptionally well-written film. (Well, except *Critters 3*, and we all have to start somewhere!) That's no accident. When Leonardo is looking to do a film, he searches for the best-written scripts he can find. It is Leo himself who makes the ultimate decision as to what films he will do, and he tends to go for movie scripts with fascinating storylines, intense character development, and expressive dialogue. Sometimes that means turning down roles in movies that are sure to be huge moneymakers, like the role of Robin in *Batman Forever.*

On these next few pages you'll find classic lines from the scripts of Leonardo's movies. Can you figure out which movie each line is from? (Beware. We've snuck in a few lines from Leo's days on the TV series Growing Pains.*)*

1. "My mom had high hopes, especially for me. I've been giving her no end of grief since she left Dad. I decided I was going to do better. I was gonna have straight-arrow friends, I was gonna get all As in school, and I was gonna keep my nose clean. I promised it, and I meant it."

2. "I've never had a date. When you live on the streets you don't go out. You are out."

3. "How about getting together sometime and doing something normal?"

4. "Der my hoppers. Der my friends."

5. "I've known Bobby since I was three. He's my best friend. He was the best player on our basketball team. Two years ago, he got leukemia. He keeps fighting it off. I know Bobby's gonna beat it. He can beat anything."

6. "Do I hear cluckin'? Did someone bring a chicken in here?"

7. "Don't expect me to be faithful to you."

8. "I'm the king of the world!"

9. "I can't. I'm involved now. You let go and I'll have to jump in after you."

10. "Did my heart love 'til now? For swear it, sight. I ne'er saw true beauty 'til this night."

11. "I would have thought it was impossible, but I do believe the excitement of this whole chase has made you even more beautiful."

12. "I think I missed the homecoming dance. I believe that was the night I was out looking through a dumpster for shoes."

13. "Yeah, Mom, I'm up. The loony alarm went off."

14. "Whoa now. What if someone gets too excited and starts shootin' early?"

15. "Mom, I'm really sorry I burned the house down."

16. "Anyway, one time I fell through some thin ice and let me tell you, that water is cold. Hits you like a thousand knives stabbing you all over your body. You can't breathe, you can't think . . . at least about anything but the pain."

17. "This I pray, that thou consent to marry us today."

18. "Riots! But Paris is the most beautiful city in the world. Why should my people feel anything but pride and contentment?"

19. "I looked at his body and it was death for the first time. His face was thin and wrinkled, almost ape-like. He looked sixty years old and he was sixteen. I couldn't believe how skinny he was, much skinnier than he was when he was in the hospital. It was like having a skeleton of someone you knew put right in front of you. I felt dazed just like I came out of a four-hour movie I didn't understand."

20. "Is he that guy that comes down from the boondocks? The mechanic? Dwight. What a stupid name."

21. "Don't call me sport."

22. "My mom wants me to become eighteen and I'm having a big, big party."

23. "The gunfight is in the head, not the hands. The only thing that makes him invincible is because you all think he is. Maybe five years ago he was the fastest, but time catches up with everyone."

24. "Well, you know they crawl out of the drain in the boy's shower. Sometimes they like to hide in the junk pile in the auto shop. They like float around in the soap basins in the sink. You get used to them."

25. "Whatever it is that binds families and married couples together is not love. It's stupidity or selfishness or fear. Love doesn't exist."

26. "I've been in prison for six years. You have freed me, but now you are asking me to enter another prison."

27. "Your nose is running, your stomach cramps, your legs feel like they've played six straight games on top of each other. And the voice is always there in the back of your head. 'Just one more time, then we'll stop.' And you wanna stop. You really do, but it's like a dream."

28. "A lot can happen in two years. Skipper and Norman left Concrete and moved to Seattle. I was going to get out too, for sure."

29. "And that's the story of Flat Nosed Foy who currently resides six feet under."

30. "I was thinking, what could have happened to this girl to make her think she had no way out."

31. "No thanks. I like to eat alone. By the way, you'll be leaving tomorrow."

32. "This morning I wasn't on the street. I had a place to sleep and a place to eat and a promising academic career."

33. "Do you love him?"

34. "Of all the wonders I have seen, I've never looked upon anything as beautiful as you."

35. "Are they gonna come soon? 'Cause I gotta go back home, ya know."

36. "It ain't about that. I'm his son and if this is the only way he's gonna admit that then so be it."

37. "The only unbearable thing is that nothing is unbearable."

38. "I saw that in a nickelodeon once and I always wanted to do it."

39. "I didn't know you had a sister."

40. "It means what it says. No more, no less."

ANSWERS TO THE SOUND BITES QUIZ

1. *This Boy's Life*

2. *Growing Pains*

3. *Critters 3*

4. *What's Eating Gilbert Grape*

5. *The Basketball Diaries*

6. *The Quick and the Dead*

7. *Total Eclipse*

8. *Titanic*

9. *Titanic*

10. *Romeo & Juliet*

11. *The Man in the Iron Mask*

12. *Growing Pains*

13. *The Basketball Diaries*

14. *The Quick and the Dead*

15. *Marvin's Room*

16. *Titanic*

17. *Romeo & Juliet*

18. *The Man in the Iron Mask*

19. *The Basketball Diaries*

20. *This Boy's Life*

21. *Critters 3*

22. *What's Eating Gilbert Grape*

23. *The Quick and the Dead*

24. *Marvin's Room*

25. *Total Eclipse*

26. *The Man in the Iron Mask*

27. *The Basketball Diaries*

28. *This Boy's Life*

29. *The Quick and the Dead*

30. *Titanic*

31. *The Man in the Iron Mask*

32. *Growing Pains*

33. *Titanic*

34. *The Man in the Iron Mask*

35. *What's Eating Gilbert Grape*

36. *The Quick and the Dead*

37. *Total Eclipse*

38. *Titanic*

39. *Marvin's Room*

40. *Total Eclipse*

18
THE ULTIMATE LEO
TRIVIA CHALLENGE

Warning: This quiz is not for amateurs. Only true Leonardo DiCaprio fans should continue on. We are not responsible for any injury caused by brain drain!

1. What museum was Leo's mom visiting when she was pregnant with Leonardo and decided on his name?

2. Finish the title of Leo's early educational film: *How to Deal with* _____.

3. Who was Leo's pediatrician?

4. For which film did Leo earn his first seven-figure contract?

5. Leo lost a role as a reporter in what Tom Cruise film?

6. Why did Leo lose the role named in question 5?

7. Leo spent New Year's Eve 1998 with his pals (including Sarah Gilbert) at a club owned by what movie star?

8. Of what U.S. city did Leo say, "You could probably sit in a corner all day and have a more fulfilling day than traveling all over L.A. and seeing all the sights"?

9. Leo's former love, Kristen Zang, also dated which Oscar-winning actor?

10. What is Leo's favorite James Dean film?

11. Leonardo once donated money to save what species of endangered water animals?

12. What movie did Leo see on his first date?

13. What grade was Leo in when he went on his first date?

14. What does Leo like to make with his pals when he has time off?

15. What does Leo wear in his hair to hold his bangs back?

16. During filming of *The Man in the Iron Mask*, Leo and a friend went out and did some all-

terrain-vehicle racing. Leo's pal was injured.
What bone did he break?

17. What liquid snack is Leo's mom famous for offering to his friends?

18. What is Juliette Lewis's nickname for Leonardo?

19. True or false: A Hollywood agent once turned Leo down because he didn't like his nose.

20. One of Leo's favorite possessions is a rare baseball card of what former Los Angeles Dodger?

21. Leonardo's real-estate agent is pretty famous herself. She once inspired members of the rock band The Knack to write a hit song about her. What is her name, and what was the song called?

22. What is Leo's pet lizard's name?

23. What happened to Leo's pet lizard on the set of *Titanic*?

24. For what on-line magazine did Leo write a poem called "Untitled"?

25. In 1996 Leo won an E! Entertainment Television award. What was the category he won for?

Answers to the
Ultimate Leo Trivia Challenge Quiz

1. Italy's Uffizzi Gallery

2. *A Parent Who Takes Drugs*

3. Paul Fleiss, father of the notorious Heidi Fleiss

4. *Titanic*

5. *Interview with the Vampire.* The role was supposed to go to River Phoenix, whose untimely death left the part untaken. Leo auditioned, but the part eventually went to Christian Slater.

6. He was too young.

7. Sean Penn

8. New York City

9. Nicholas Cage

10. *East of Eden*

11. Manatees

12. *When Harry Met Sally*

13. Eighth

14. He likes shooting home movies on video.

15. A thin silver wire band

16. His fibula

17. Vitamin shakes

18. My little pal

19. False. He didn't like his haircut.

20. Sandy Koufax

21. Sharona Alperin. The song was called *"My Sharona."*

22. Blizzard

23. It almost died after being run over by a truck.

24. *Totally DeCapitated*

25. Male Trendsetter of the Year

19
HOW DO YOU MEASURE UP?

Okay, here's where we separate the fans from the fanatics. Some people may have more Leo posters and others more movie videos, but only the people with the most correct answers are true DiCaprimaniacs.

Here's how to figure out your score: Start by checking your answers in each section. Then write down the number of questions you answered correctly in the corresponding spaces on the chart below. Add up your total number of correct answers and check the chart for your results.

Leo's Vital Statistics (15)   _____
Leo's Family Tree (25)   _____
Faves! (25)   _____

Meet the Co-stars (20)   _____

Leo Geo(graphy) (25)   _____

Tube Time! (30)   _____

Critters 3 (10)   _____

This Boy's Life (10)   _____

What's Eating Gilbert Grape (15)   _____

The Basketball Diaries (15)   _____

Total Eclipse (15)   _____

The Quick and the Dead (15)   _____

William Shakespeare's Romeo & Juliet (15)   _____

Marvin's Room (15)   _____

Titanic (20)   _____

The Man in the Iron Mask (15)   _____

Sound Bites (40)   _____

The Ultimate Leo Trivia Challenge (25)   _____

Total: (350)   _____

350 correct: Hey, wait a minute! There's really only one person who could get this many questions right. Hey Leo, shouldn't you be off looking for your next great movie instead of answering questions about yourself!?

260–349 correct: No doubt about it, you have reached Leo fanatic status. As far as you're concerned, Leo really is king of the world!

185–259 correct: Awesome score! You sure do know a lot about this boy's life. Keep up the good work.

100–184 correct: You are obviously a big fan of Leo's. But if you want to bring up your score quicker than a salvage crew can raise the Titanic, try having a movie marathon this weekend. (May we recommend *Titanic, The Basketball Diaries,* and *This Boy's Life* for starters?)

50–99 correct: While it's true that this is not exactly a high score, all hope has not gone the way of *Romeo & Juliet.* What you need is a little extra time with those teen magazines and a few extra trips to the video store.

1–49 correct: Yikes! You seem to have missed out on all the Leo excitement! Where have you been—imprisoned in an iron mask for the past few years? But never fear. You can catch up. For a quick refresher course go back to the beginning of this book and read through it again. Before long, you'll be a high scorer too!

About the Author

Nancy Krulik is the author of the bestselling book, *Leonardo DiCaprio: A Biography*. She has also written books on pop stars Taylor Hanson, Isaac Hanson, MC Hammer, and Vanilla Ice, as well as a new music trivia book, *Pop Quiz*. She lives in Manhattan with her husband, composer Daniel Burwasser, and their two children.

About the Author

Nancy Krulik is the author of the bestselling book, Leonardo DiCaprio: A Biography. She has also written books on pop stars Taylor Hanson, Isaac Hanson, MC Hammer, and Vanilla Ice, as well as a new chapter in the book Pop Quiz. She lives in Manhattan with her husband, composer Daniel Burwasser, and their two children.

From Archway Paperbacks

Published by Pocket Books

☆MOST WANTED: *Holiday Hunks*

A posterbook full of your favorite stars—including

- ☆Leonardo DiCaprio
- ☆Matt Damon
- ☆Hanson
- ☆Will Smith
- ☆Jakob Dylan
- ☆Freddy Prinze , Jr.
- ☆James van der Beek
- ☆Nicholas Brendon
- ☆Prince William
- ☆Tiger Woods
- ☆Jared Leto
- ☆Matt LeBlank
- ☆Scott Wolf
- ☆Aaron Carter
- ☆Seth Green
- ☆David Boreanaz

☆ The Backstreet Boys

From the worlds of television, sports, music, and big-screen movies, these POSTER BOYS are ready to go up on your locker, walls, or note-books—anywhere you want to catch a glimpse of these babes!

Coming in mid-November 1998

From Archway Paperbacks
Published by Pocket Books

2020

LEONARDO DICAPRIO
A Biography

By Nancy Krulik

Make sure you have the book with all the info on the hot star of *Titanic* and *The Man in the Iron Mask*, plus eight pages of color photos!

POCKET BOOKS

Available from Pocket Books

THE HOTTEST STARS
THE BEST BIOGRAPHIES

☆ **Hanson: MMMBop to the Top** ☆
By Jill Mattthews

☆ **Hanson: The Ultimate Trivia Book!** ☆
By Matt Netter

☆ **Isaac Hanson: Totally Ike!** ☆
By Nancy Krulik

☆ **Taylor Hanson: Totally Taylor!** ☆
By Nancy Krulik

☆ **Zac Hanson: Totally Zac!** ☆
By Matt Netter

☆ **Jonathan Taylor Thomas:
Totally JTT!** ☆
By Michael-Anne Johns

☆ **Leonardo DiCaprio: A Biography** ☆
By Nancy Krulik

☆ **Will Power!
A Biography of Will Smith** ☆
By Jan Berenson

☆ **Prince William:
The Boy Who Will Be King** ☆
By Randi Reisfeld

Available from Archway Paperbacks
Published by Pocket Books

1491